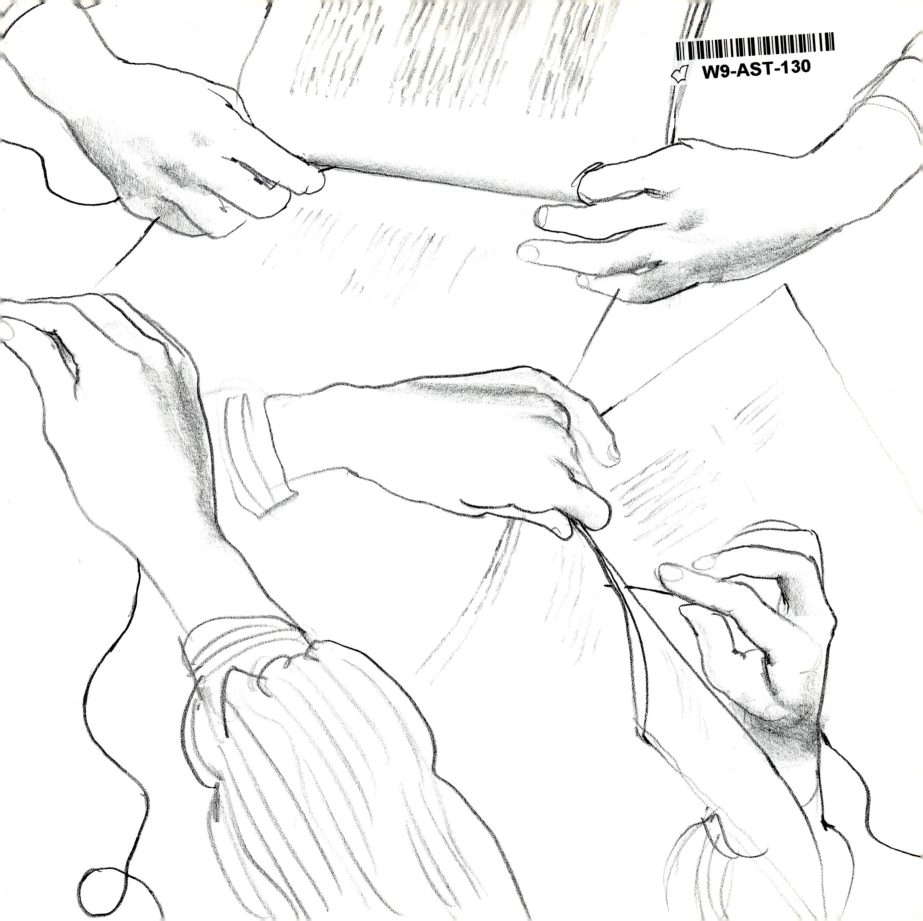

Anna

— the —

BOOKBINDER

WALKER & COMPANY

NEW YORK

Andrea Cheng

illustrations by
Ted Rand

First published in the United States of America in 2003 by
Walker Publishing Company, Inc.

Published simultaneously in Canada by Fitzhenry and Whiteside,
Markham, Ontario L3R 4T8

For information about permission to reproduce selections from
this book, write to Permissions, Walker & Company, 435 Hudson
Street, New York, New York 10014

Library of Congress Cataloging-in-Publication Data
available upon request
ISBN 0-8027-8831-9(hardcover)
ISBN 0-8027-8832-7(reinforced)

The illustrations for this book were created using transparent watercolor
on 100 percent rag stock.

Book design by Diane Hobbing of Snap-Haus Graphics

Visit Walker & Company's Web site at www.walkerbooks.com

Printed in Hong Kong

10 9 8 7 6 5 4 3 2 1

To Jane, with love.
—A. C.

To Beth and Jack Bakke,
the book lovers.
—T. R.

y papa smells like paper and leather and glue. When I sit on his lap at night I find paper snippets in his hair. He lets me peel the dry glue from his fingertips.

We live upstairs. Downstairs is our book bindery, with its big presses and paper cutters, where Papa works on books all day, and even into the night.

Lately Papa is tired. He says the libraries are taking their books to big binderies that can work faster than one binder all by himself. People don't know that they use glue instead of stitches to bind the books. They don't know that the glue will get hard and the books' spines will crack.

ven Papa's biggest client, Mr. Levinson, is threatening to take his business elsewhere. Yesterday he brought in a three-volume set.

"How long will it take you to finish these?" he asked.

Papa looked each volume over. "A week, Mr. Levinson," he said.

"A whole week? I need them in three days for my wife's birthday."

"I'll try to finish them in time," Papa said, sighing.

"Three days, then," said Mr. Levinson, turning to leave. "If you can't do it, let me know, and I'll run them over to Solomon's bindery."

I wanted to tell Mr. Levinson that Solomon's bindery would ruin his books, but Papa told me to go upstairs.

ama is tired, too, with her stomach full of my new baby brother or sister. The baby was supposed to be born a week ago, but it doesn't seem to be in a hurry. That's why we call it our tortoise. After breakfast, I follow Papa down to the bindery and watch his hands, so strong and sure, working a rectangle of yellow leather.

"Is that for one of Mr. Levinson's books?"

"No, Anna, this is one I started before. *Fables* by Aesop. Do you remember Aesop?"

"The one who wrote about the tortoise and the hare?" I ask.

Papa smiles. "That's right."

Then he works quietly, leaning his weight into the knife and shaving off curls of leather that fall onto the floor. I collect them into a pile. When he is done, Papa puts Aesop into the big press and tightens it until all that shows is the spine. I want to take it out and read the old stories, but I have to wait.

hile Papa works, I sit underneath the bench, far out of the way. There I find my pile of yellow curled leather. I make another pile of scraps of paper, then one of string. I look over at Aesop, pressed so tightly he can hardly breathe. It's okay, I want to tell him, tomorrow you will open and close again like new.

While Aesop is in the press and Papa is working on Mr. Levinson's books, I play around with the scraps. I arrange them on a piece of cardboard this way and that. Slowly a picture emerges of a forest with a path through it. Then I make a hare asleep behind a boulder, and a tortoise so far ahead he is almost off the cardboard.

ama calls us for lunch, but Papa says he is too busy and that we should eat without him. After lunch, I go with Mama to the corner store to buy bread and milk. She can only take tiny steps, her stomach is so big. I carry our packages.

ll afternoon I work on my picture. When it is just the way I want it, I glue everything down. But the bottom still looks empty. I know, I'll write the moral there: Slow but steady wins the race. It takes a long time to cut the string into letters, but when it is done, I am pleased. I smile, thinking what Aesop would say if he could see it. Tomorrow, before he goes back to his owner, I will read him. Papa always lets me do that.

t night Mama says I smell just like Papa. "Anna, why do you stay in the workshop all day? Why don't you play outside?" She sighs. Papa, too. He has to go back downstairs; there is still work to do. Mama nods. She knows about Mr. Levinson. She bends down to say good night, but her stomach is so big she cannot reach me.

hen I wake up, there is a note from Papa on my night table. "Dear Anna, we are upstairs with the midwife, waiting for our tortoise. I will come and tell you as soon as it arrives. Please open the press for me. Love, Papa." I tiptoe downstairs. The bindery is dark and quiet. I hold the big press wheel firmly in my hands. First it will not turn. I know it is important not to leave a book in the press too long, so I lean all my weight into the wheel. When it finally moves, I fall and scrape my knee, but Aesop is free.

I hold the book carefully and open the front cover to the first page. "The Stories of Aesop," it says. Then on the blank page opposite, Papa has written, "To Anna and our new baby tortoise. Love, Papa."

can hardly believe it! I never thought that with all his other work, Papa was binding a book for me. I want to read Aesop right away, but there is work to be done. I clean off the workbench like Papa does each morning. There on the side are Mr. Levinson's three books, ready to be stitched.

I've seen Papa do it often. I've even stitched some blank books for myself. But will Papa be angry? What if the thread gets tangled? What if our new baby tortoise takes a long time to arrive, and Mr. Levinson's books are not ready for his wife's birthday? Then his hard blue eyes will look right through Papa, and he will take his books away.

run the thread through beeswax first to keep it from tangling. Then I begin to re-stitch the first volume, pulling the thread tight at the end of each row. I go back and forth through all the pages of the book. When my thread is too short, I tie a knot and begin again. I want to have all three of Mr. Levinson's books ready by the time our tortoise arrives.

ust as I finish the last book, I hear footsteps on the stairs. There is Papa. "It's a boy!" he says. His name is Robert. Papa says his hair is black like mine. Then Papa sees the three books.

"You re-stitched all of them already?"

I look at Papa's face, worried that he might be mad. But he isn't. He is fingering the spines proudly. "The stitches are tight, and you remembered the beeswax," he says.

"Mr. Levinson will have his books in time for his wife's birthday," I say.

hen Papa's eyes catch my picture still underneath the workbench.

"Anna, it's beautiful," he says, holding it upright.

"It's for Robert," I say.

"Maybe Robert will let me borrow it for the front door of the workshop. That way, when people bring their books to us, they'll know that we are like the tortoise. We may not be fast, but we do a good job."

At night Mama lets me hold Robert all by myself. I can see the swirls on his tiny fingertips. I wonder if someday they will be covered in glue like mine and Papa's. I show him the picture, and he opens his eyes for a minute. Then I hand him to Mama and read him "The Tortoise and the Hare" from our very own book. Papa stands above me and plucks a snippet of paper from my hair. It floats slowly to the floor as I read.

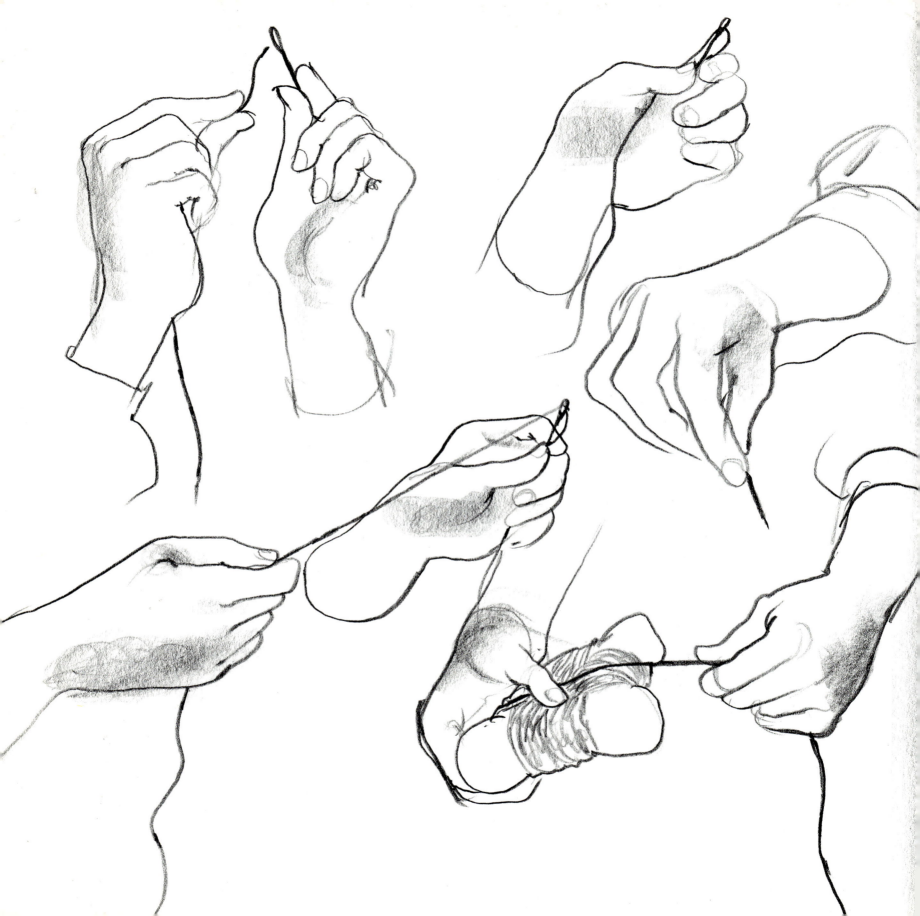